This series of stories is designed to be read aloud to very young children. Each story, whether about familiar experiences, or just fantasy, has been beautifully and carefully illustrated so that the pictures themselves tell the story. The simple storyline will direct the young child's attention to the pictures. Slightly older children, who are beginning to read, will enjoy reading the story themselves, helped by the colourful illustrations.

Also available in Series S811

A Fly in his Eye

Oliver Octopus

Lost in the Supermarket

The Weathervane

Tommy's Tuba

First Edition

The Fastest Snail on Earth

written by MOIRA SMITH

illustrated by KEITH LOGAN

Ladybird Books Loughborough

Sidney is a snail.

He has his home on his back.

Sidney moves very, very slowly.

Because he moves slowly, he sees many beautiful things.

But Sidney wishes he could move faster.

He often daydreams. He dreams he is an aeroplane.

Sometimes he dreams he is the first snail on the moon.

But most often Sidney dreams he is a racing car.

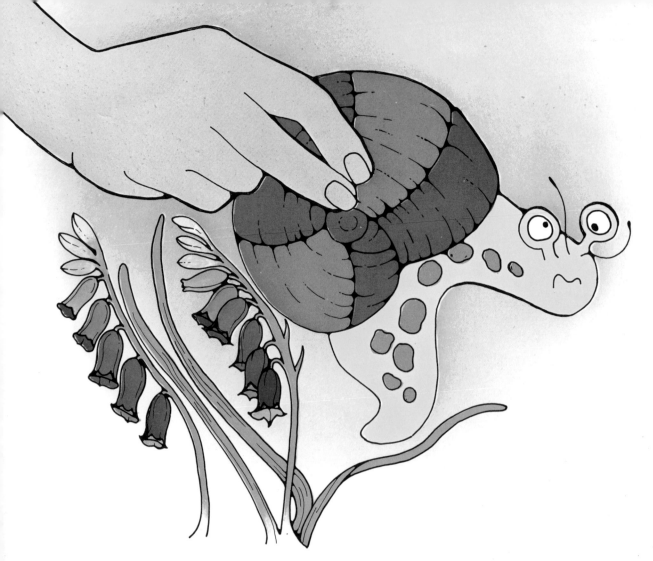

One day he was moving along, very slowly, looking for
a lettuce leaf. Suddenly he was flying through the air.

"Am I flying, or am I dreaming?" said Sidney.
A little boy called Andrew had picked up Sidney.

"I won't hurt you, Mr Snail," said Andrew.
"Look, these are my cars."

Sidney saw the racing car of his dreams.

Andrew put Sidney into a car.

"Vroom! Vroom!" said Andrew and he drove the car
round and round.

The car went faster and faster. "You're the fastest snail on earth!" shouted Andrew.

"Oooah!" moaned Sidney. "This must be
a very bad dream."

Sidney thought of his Mum. She always said, "If snails
needed to go fast, they would have wheels."

His Mum was right. "I never want to go fast again,"
thought Sidney.

Round went the car until Sidney was very dizzy.
"Please stop," he said.

"You're the winner!" shouted Andrew. And the car stopped at last.

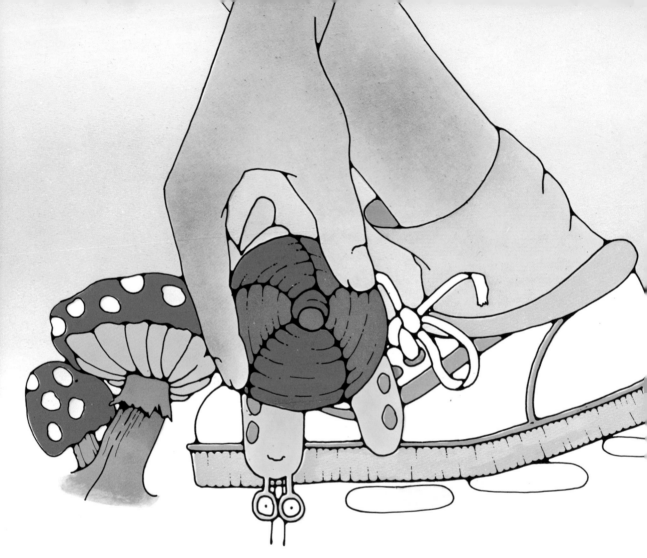

Andrew picked up Sidney and put him down
where he found him.

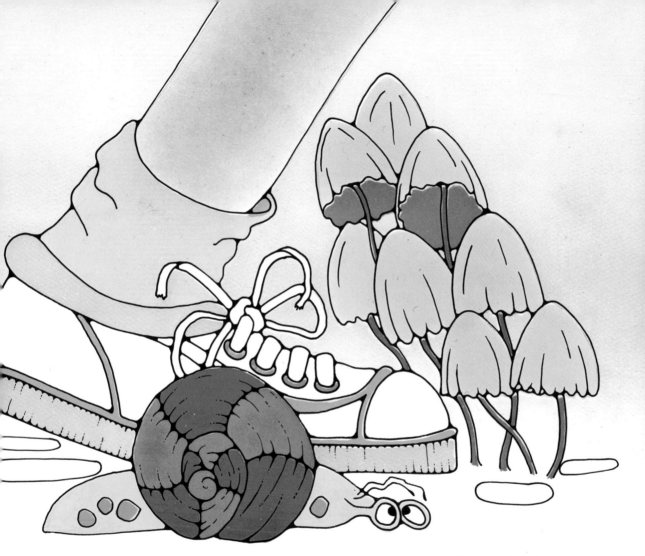

"Goodbye, Mr Snail," he said, and he went into the house.

Sidney ate a lettuce leaf and then went into his shell.
He was very, very tired.